MODERN CURRICULUM PRESS

Robin Drake, A Robot

Joy Ann Tweedt
Craig L. Tweedt
Alvin Granowsky
Illustrated by Michael L. Denman

MODERN CURRICULUM PRESS
Cleveland • Toronto

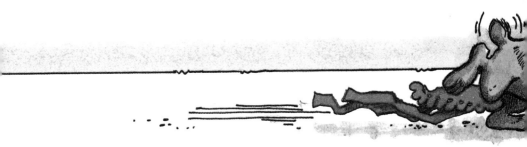

© **1986 MODERN CURRICULUM PRESS, INC.**
13900 Prospect Road, Cleveland, Ohio 44136.

Softcover edition published simultaneously in Canada by Globe/
Modern Curriculum Press, Toronto.

Library of Congress Cataloging in Publication Data

Tweedt, Joy Ann, 1951-
  Robin Drake, a robot.

  Summary: Robin the robot is a great help with her family's
household chores, until a fall damages a microchip and scram-
bles her programming.
  1. Children's stories, American. (1. Robots — Fiction.
2. Science fiction)   I. Tweedt, Craig L., 1950-   .
II. Granowsky, Alvin, 1936-   .   III. Denman, Michael L.,
ill.   IV. Title.
PZ7.T897Ro   1985   (E)   85-8834

ISBN 0-8136-5165-4
ISBN 0-8136-5665-6 (pbk.)

1 2 3 4 5 6 7 8 9 10   87 86 85

"Breakfast is ready, Tracy," called Mrs. Drake. Tracy hurried to the kitchen. There she saw Robin putting a plate of bacon and eggs on the table.

Robin was the Drake family's robot.
Tracy named her Robin because of the
chirping sounds Robin made as she
worked.

"Mmmm! That smells great, Mom!" said
Tracy as she sat down to eat.

6

7

"Robin cooked the eggs this morning,"
said Mrs. Drake. "And they do taste good."
As Tracy took a bite, she was sure she
saw a twinkle in Robin's eyes.

CHIRP TWEET CHIRP

9

"Robin, please press Tracy's blouse," asked Mrs. Drake.

Tracy watched as Robin rolled out of the kitchen.

CHIRP CHIRP♪

Robin was a big help to the Drake family. She always washed the dishes and put them neatly on the shelf.

Robin ran the carpet sweeper and dusted the furniture.

She fed and walked the dog, cut and raked the grass, and washed and waxed the car.

Robin could do almost anything, from cooking dinner to shoveling snow in the winter.

Robin could be fun, too. Many times Robin would read a book to Tracy. Sometimes they would play ball in the yard.

Robin had become a member of the Drake family.

Tracy finished eating and then dressed for school. As she walked down the sidewalk, she heard Robin chirping behind her.

CHIRP CHIRP CHIRP CHIRP CHIRP CHIRP

Tracy turned around. She saw Robin carrying the school books Tracy had forgotten. Robin was rolling too fast. Poor Robin slipped and fell.

Tracy ran to help Robin. "Oh, Robin!" cried Tracy, "I hope you're not broken."

Robin chirped softly. She got up slowly and handed the books to Tracy.

"Thank you, Robin. I'm glad you're not broken."

Tracy gave Robin a hug, pointed her toward the house, and then walked to school.

When Tracy got home, she knew
something was wrong.

"I just don't know what to do!" cried
Mrs. Drake. "Robin is just not herself!"

"This morning Robin washed the dog and put him on the shelf."

"Then she fed the carpet sweeper and took it for a walk."

"Robin took the dirty dishes and hung them on the clothesline."

"Then she put the clean clothes into the dishwasher."

"Robin raked the car and waxed the lawn mower."

25

"Oh, no!" cried Tracy. "This morning
Robin fell down the steps. She must be
broken."

"We must take Robin to be repaired,"
said Mrs. Drake.

Mrs. Drake and Tracy took Robin to the robot repair shop. Robin stayed there for three long days.

The Drakes missed Robin. Things just weren't the same around the house.

The people at the repair shop fixed Robin's dents and replaced one of her computer chips. She was now ready to go home.

SURPRISE! WELCOME HOM

When Robin rolled into the house, the
Drakes all yelled,
"WELCOME HOME, ROBIN!"

CHIRP
CHIRP

CHIRRRP ♫

Tracy looked closely at Robin's face. She
was sure that she saw a twinkle in
Robin's eyes.